ELITE FORCES SURVIVAL GUIDES

SURVIVE IN THE WILDERNESS WITH THE CANADIAN AND AUSTRALIAN SPECIAL FORCES

ELITE FORCES SURVIVAL GUIDE SERIES

Elite Survival
Survive in the Desert with the French Foreign Legion
Survive in the Arctic with the Royal Marine Commandos
Survive in the Mountains with the U.S. Rangers and Army
  Mountain Division
Survive in the Jungle with the Special Forces "Green Berets"
Survive in the Wilderness with the Canadian and Australian
  Special Forces
Survive at Sea with the U.S. Navy SEALs
Training to Fight with the Parachute Regiment
The World's Best Soldiers

Elite Operations and Training
Escape and Evasion
Surviving Captivity with the U.S. Air Force
Hostage Rescue with the SAS
How to Pass Elite Forces Selection
Learning Mental Endurance with the U.S. Marines

Special Forces Survival Guidebooks
Survival Equipment
Navigation and Signaling
Surviving Natural Disasters
Using Ropes and Knots
Survival First Aid
Trapping, Fishing, and Plant Food
Urban Survival Techniques

SURVIVE IN THE WILDERNESS WITH THE CANADIAN AND AUSTRALIAN SPECIAL FORCES

CHRIS McNAB

Introduction by Colonel John T. Carney. Jr., USAF–Ret.
President, Special Operations Warrior Foundation

MASON CREST PUBLISHERS

This edition first published in 2003
by Mason Crest Publishers Inc.
370 Reed Road, Broomall, PA, 19008

Library of Congress Cataloging-in-Publication Data available

ISBN 1-59084-005-4

Editorial and design by
Amber Books Ltd.
Bradley's Close
74–77 White Lion Street
London N1 9PF

Project Editor Chris Stone
Designer Simon Thompson
Picture Research Lisa Wren

Printed and bound in Malaysia

10 9 8 7 6 5 4 3 2 1

ACKNOWLEDGMENT
For authenticating this book, the Publishers would like to thank the Public Affairs Offices of the U.S. Special Operations Command, MacDill AFB, FL.; Army Special Operations Command, Fort Bragg, N.C.; Navy Special Warfare Command, Coronado, CA.; and the Air Force Special Operations Command, Hurlbert Field, FL.

IMPORTANT NOTICE
The survival techniques and information described in this publication are for use in dire circumstances where the safety of the individual is at risk. Accordingly, the publisher cannot accept any responsibility for any prosecution or proceedings brought or instituted against any person or body as a result of the uses or misuses of the techniques and information within.

DEDICATION
This book is dedicated to those who perished in the terrorist attacks of September 11, 2001, and to the Special Forces soldiers who continually serve to defend freedom.

Picture Credits
Australian Army: 23, 82, 84; **Corbis**: 6, 47, 63, 71, 74, 76, 78; **Dept. of National Defense, Canada**: 36, 81; **TRH**: 8, 14, 15, 16, 18, 22, 24, 28, 29, 31, 34, 37, 42, 50, 52, 60, 62, 64, 68, 70
Illustrations courtesy of; Amber Books, De Agostini UK and the following supplied by Patrick Mulrey: 27, 40, 44, 57
Front cover: **Australian Army** (inset), **TRH** (main)

CONTENTS

Introduction 6

The History of the Regiments 8

What to Wear 16

What to Carry 24

Water 34

Fire 42

Food 50

Shelter 60

Improvising Tools and Weapons 68

Rescue 76

Dangers 84

Glossary 90

Equipment Requirements 92

Chronology 93

Recruitment Information 94

Further Reading/About the Author 95

Index 96

INTRODUCTION

Elite forces are the tip of Freedom's spear. These small, special units are universally the first to engage, whether on reconnaissance missions into denied territory for larger, conventional forces or in direct action, surgical operations, preemptive strikes, retaliatory action, and hostage rescues. They lead the way in today's war on terrorism, the war on drugs, the war on transnational unrest, and in humanitarian operations as well as nation building. When large scale warfare erupts, they offer theater commanders a wide variety of unique, unconventional options.

Most such units are regionally oriented, acclimated to the culture and conversant in the languages of the areas where they operate. Since they deploy to those areas regularly, often for combined training exercises with indigenous forces, these elite units also serve as peacetime "global scouts" and "diplomacy multipliers," a beacon of hope for the democratic aspirations of oppressed peoples all over the globe.

Elite forces are truly "quiet professionals": their actions speak louder than words. They are self-motivated, self-confident, versatile, seasoned, mature individuals who rely on teamwork more than daring-do. Unfortunately, theirs is dangerous work. Since "Desert One"—the 1980 attempt to rescue hostages from the U.S. embassy in Tehran, for instance—American special operations forces have suffered casualties in real world operations at close to fifteen times the rate of U.S. conventional forces. By the very nature of the challenges which face special operations forces, training for these elite units has proven even more hazardous.

Thus it's with special pride that I join you in saluting the brave men and women who volunteer to serve in and support these magnificent units and who face such difficult challenges ahead.

Colonel John T. Carney, Jr., USAF–Ret.
President, Special Operations Warrior Foundation

An elite soldier takes part in a wilderness survival course. Given very little provisions, he must fend for himself in extreme conditions.

THE HISTORY OF THE REGIMENTS

If you need to know how to survive in the wilderness, go to the experts. In the world of elite forces, there are few units that have greater survival talents than the Canadian Special Forces and Australian Special Air Service (SAS). Both have to operate in the harshest wilderness environments.

All soldiers in modern armies have to be trained in survival skills. But why? There are several reasons: they could be cut off from their units far behind enemy lines; they could run out of food and supplies; they could be exposed to severe weather or environments. In any of these situations soldiers will need survival skills to keep themselves alive, living off the land and protecting themselves from the elements.

Yet some elite units need survival skills more than most. The Canadian Special Forces and the Australian **SAS** are two such units. Both have to cope with incredibly tough environments. The Australian SAS must survive in the barren landscape of the Australian outback, where temperatures are extremely hot, food is scarce, and they are surrounded by dangerous wildlife. (Australia has more types of poisonous animal than any other country in the world—snakes and spiders are among the most common.) By contrast, the

An Australian SAS team on patrol in Vietnam in 1969. The gun they carry is the extremely popular 7.62-mm caliber FN FAL rifle.

Canadian Special Forces have to survive in the wildernesses of Canada, with winter temperatures plummeting to –34°F (–40°C) and snow drifts climbing to many feet in height.

The demands of surviving in these two environments are not as different as you might think. Both units have the same priorities: finding food and water, making shelter, avoiding dangerous animals, and knowing how to treat themselves for illnesses and injuries. Not only have these elite units tested their skills in their own countries, but their missions have also taken them into combat around the world. Consequently, they are among the world's best authorities on the art of wilderness survival.

The Australian SAS was born in World War II (1939–1945) when it seemed as if the Japanese might invade Australia itself. The Australians knew that they were experts at fighting and surviving in the arid bush and deserts. So special units were raised in July 1942 to patrol into remote, unmapped areas of the northern coast and report on enemy movements. Some groups actually fought the Japanese in the jungles of the Pacific.

At the end of the war, most of these units were disbanded. But elite units were soon needed again for other wars, and in 1957 the 1st Australian SAS company was created. The primary role of the new SAS unit was reconnaissance, inserting parachutists deep into enemy territory to gather intelligence.

The badge of the Canadian First Special Service Force, 1942.

They spent the next few years training in the hostile terrain of northwestern Australia, having to exist in the scorching sun, and having to fight crocodiles and sharks instead of enemy soldiers. Here, they gained excellent survival skills.

The Australian SAS troops were soon fighting in Borneo alongside the British and New Zealand SAS. They proved that they were excellent soldiers, and soon showed that they were worthy of the elite name. In Borneo, they did everything that the British SAS was doing—conducting dangerous combat missions right into the heart of the Bornean jungle. In 1966, the unit found itself involved with a new war in Vietnam, this time fighting alongside the United States. After major battles between regular Australian and communist soldiers (called the **Viet Cong**, or VC), four-

An Australian special forces soldier in Vietnam, wearing the distinctive "Tiger Stripe" camouflage pattern adopted by U.S. forces during the war.

or five-man SAS patrols searched for parties of VC who had survived. During the **Vietnam War** there were many firefights, but usually the SAS were victorious. The Australian and New Zealand SAS killed more than 500 enemy for the loss of one man and 27 wounded during a five-year period. The communists were very respectful of them. They called them Ma Rung or "jungle ghosts"; they put a price on their heads of $5,000 a man, dead or alive.

Since Vietnam, the Australian SAS has been in constant training. Like other modern elite forces, they are now experts in fighting terrorism as well as battles on open ground. There is a special Training Squadron that is responsible for selection and advanced training.

The Australian SAS wears standard Australian Army uniforms with the distinctive sand-colored beret and the famous winged dagger SAS badge. British Special Air Service-type parachute wings are usually worn on the right upper sleeve.

The story of the Canadian Special Forces is in many ways similar. Elite Canadian forces

A soldier of the Princess Patricia's Light Infantry, one of Canada's most prestigious units.

were born, like so many other elite units, during World War II. Two in particular were created: the 1st Canadian Parachute Battalion and the Special Service Force. The Parachute Battalion was an elite airborne unit that trained in the United States but fought alongside the British Paras throughout the vicious battles for occupied Europe. From the invasion of France to the fall of Germany itself, the Canadian paras gained a reputation for being a tough unit to beat. The same could be said of the Special Service Force. This was actually a joint U.S.–Canadian unit, and its battleground was Italy and northern Europe. It was created on July 10, 1942, and served valiantly until the end of the war.

After the war, there were many changes among Special Forces units, and many elite units were disbanded. Yet Canada has not stood still. Over the last 50 years, it has created an elite body of troops, which includes the Canadian Special Air Service Company, the Mobile Striking Force, and the Defense Force of Canada. Canada's biggest elite unit is the Special Service Force. This is actually made up of several different units, but the largest part is actually the Canadian Airborne Regiment.

The Special Service Force is incredibly highly trained in the arts of survival, and part of its responsibility is responding to civilian disasters in remote areas. In combat, troops must be able to survive in terrain ranging from the lush woodlands of southern Canada in the summer, to the arctic conditions of northern Canada. Canada is a vast country, so its elite units have to be able to live for long periods of time without any help or resources. Luckily, Canada has plentiful supplies of natural food and water. Yet the weather can be so extreme, particularly in the winter, that it takes a tough breed of soldier to survive. The Para or SAS units might be dropped into the wilderness, and not see supplies for many days, so unless they can live off the land, they are in big trouble.

All members of the Special Service Force wear a badge similar to that worn by the British SAS. It features a winged dagger and the motto "Who Dares." This motto is a good example of the spirit that is found in all elite units, including the Australian SAS. To survive in the wilderness takes someone who can dare the elements to do their worst, but still keep a level head and focus on the right way to survive. In this book, the Canadian Special Forces and the Australian SAS will teach us how to do just that.

Soldiers from the Canadian Royal Army, 22nd Regiment, during peacekeeping operations in Bosnia, October 1996.

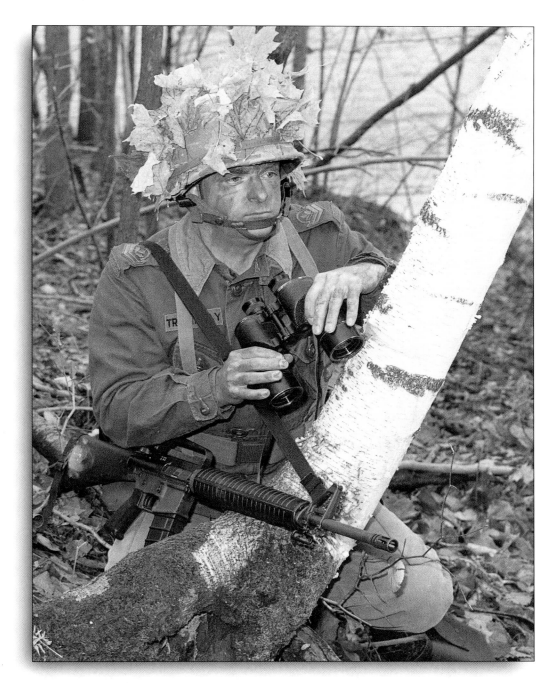

A Canadian soldier bearing an M16 rifle keeps watch during
wilderness survival training. The leaves in his helmet will provide
excellent camouflage cover when crawling along the woodland floor.

WHAT TO WEAR

The soldiers of the Canadian and Australian Special Forces need clothing that will withstand hostile weather and terrain. This chapter explains the principles they teach for selecting clothing for backpacking in wild areas.

If you have just survived a plane crash or similar accident, the chances are that you will be dressed in light, comfortable clothes that are totally unsuitable for survival situations. This being the case, you must improvise. However, if you are a backpacker or adventurer, you should be better clothed and equipped to deal with a survival situation. There is really no excuse for wearing inappropriate clothing and carrying poor equipment. Today, there is an amazing variety of clothing available to the backpacker. Above all, you must select the proper clothing for the job.

But how do you know how to equip yourself? Simple: read this book, go through magazines dedicated to outdoor pursuits, go to camping exhibitions, go to camping and survival stores, and talk to the staff who have a knowledge about such things. In short, like members of the Canadian and Australian Special Forces, find out about your operation before you set out. By doing this, you will not find out the hard way that your clothing is totally unsuitable for the wilderness.

A thick, waterproof jacket, insulating hat, and stout walking boots are an essential part of any wilderness survival kit.

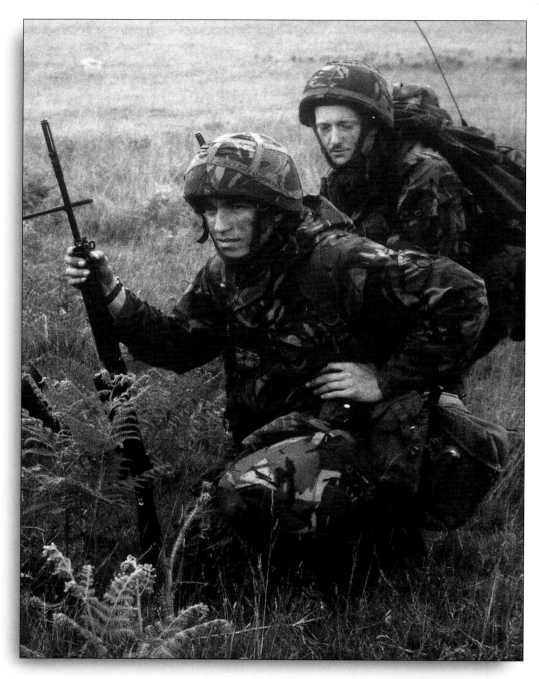

These soldiers are wearing a pattern of camouflage known as Disruptive Pattern Material (DPM). This was developed for the British Army as its standard camouflage pattern.

Gore-Tex® is an excellent material for outdoor clothing. It is a "breathable" material. This means that it lets tiny drops of sweat exit but prevents water from entering. Such amazing material is not cheap, but what price do you put on your life? Of course, just wearing a Gore-Tex® jacket is not enough. In the wilderness, the weather can go from bright, hot sunshine to freezing winds in a matter of hours, particularly if you are on a remote hillside or deep in an isolated woodland. That is why you should follow what the world's Special Forces and survival experts call "the layer principle."

The layer principle is very simple. The more layers of clothing you wear, the warmer you will be. Temperature control is very easy. If you are too hot, take off clothes; if you are too cold, put on clothes. Remember, getting too hot can be as much of a problem as being too cold. If you sweat when it is cold, the body chills when you stop sweating, and your sweat-soaked clothing will draw away body heat into the air. It is important that you prevent this. Here are the layers you should wear:

- Next to the skin, you should wear **thermal clothing**.
- Over this, wear a woolen or wool mixture shirt.
- On top of this, wear a woolen or good fiber-pile sweater, jacket, or fleece.
- As a final layer, choose a warm windproof and waterproof jacket. This should be made out of Gore-Tex® or a similar material.

Footwear

Footwear is incredibly important to soldiers in the Canadian and Australian Special Forces. For any outdoor activity, it is best to equip

CARING FOR YOUR BOOTS

As they have to march everywhere on foot, often over long distances, Canadian and Australian soldiers have good rules for the care of their boots.

- Stuff wet boots with newspaper and dry them in a warm, airy place. Do not dry them over a fire. This will bake and then crack the leather.
- Your boots should be of a size that lets you wear two or three pairs of socks underneath.
- Socks that are too tight will restrict the blood flowing to your feet. This can lead to frozen feet.
- Always carry a spare pair of socks.
- Whenever feet get wet, change socks as quickly as possible.

yourself with a pair of strong, waterproof boots high enough to support your ankles, never running shoes. It is important to look after your boots, and it is always wise to carry a spare pair of laces around with you.

Keep the boots supple and waterproof with a coating of wax or polish. Always check your boots before you use them for broken seals, worn-out treads, cracked leather, rotten stitching, and broken fastening hooks. There is no reason why you will not be able to get up to 10 years of use out of your boots if you take care of them. Many soldiers protect their boots further by wearing nylon gaiters over them to help keep water out when walking through wet grass and snow.

Socks are another important item of footwear. Most backpackers wear two pairs of socks on their feet for comfort and to prevent blisters. Whether you wear a thin pair and a thick pair, two thin pairs, or two thick pairs, is up to you. Find a combination you are happy with.

Pants

In terms of pants, you should have two pairs. The inner pair should be windproof, and the outer pair should be waterproof. The waterproof pair fit over your pants and should have a side zipper to let them be put on if you are wearing a pair of boots.

Jacket

Your jacket must be both windproof and waterproof. It should have a large hood (you can wear a hat underneath it) that protects all of your head, including the chin. The sleeves should have wrist fasteners to stop your body heat escaping, and it should be long enough to cover the tops of the thighs. It should also draw tight at the bottom and around the waist. Remember to choose a big one— you will have to wear lots of other clothing underneath it if the weather turns cold.

Gloves and hat

Finally, complete your clothing with a good pair of gloves and a hat. Both should be made of thermal material. The hat is especially important, as much of your body heat is lost through your head in cold weather. Pick something that covers your scalp, ears, forehead, and the back of your neck. One that stands up from the top of your head can be good as the space traps warm air.

All of this clothing is designed to protect you if the weather drops cold. This tends to be the most serious in wilderness settings. If weather gets hot, then there is usually plenty of shelter, and water is often easy to find in woodland, mountainous, or hilly regions. Also, you can take clothes off if you are too warm, but you cannot put them on if you do not have them. Adopt the same procedures as the Canadian and Australian Special Forces—prepare for anything.

Canadian military cold-weather clothing is some of the most advanced in the world. The Lightweight Thermal Gloves, for instance, protects soldiers in temperatures up to −86°F (−57°C).

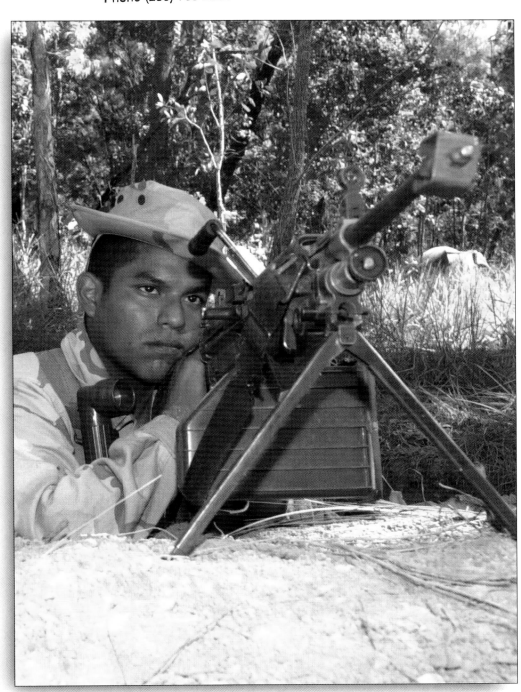

Australian uniforms reflect the terrain of the Australian wilderness. This soldier's gun has a blank firing device fitted on the muzzle.

WHAT TO CARRY

For a Special Forces soldiers on a survival mission, a few key items can mean the difference between life and death. All travelers should carry the right equipment to help them overcome any disasters that they may face.

The Canadian and Australian armies have a simple rule: do not carry useless weight. No one would consider carrying bricks and other useless weight in their backpack. However, if you have a tent, for example, that is totally unsuitable for the terrain you are in, you are carrying around dead weight. Why carry around bulky cans of food when you can have lightweight packets of nutritious **dehydrated food**? You should carry only those things that help you to survive.

The survival tin can be one of your most useful pieces of equipment. If you are equipped with the items listed below, your chances of survival are much better, whatever the terrain or weather conditions. These items of equipment are not expensive or complicated. They can be fitted into any small tin. Get used to carrying the tin around with you at all times. (It can easily fit into most jacket pockets.) Pack the contents with cotton wool—it insulates the contents and stops it rattling and, because cotton wool is flammable, it can also be used for making fire.

The standard backpack for many armies is the bergen. All the clothing and perishables inside should be sealed in waterproof bags.

Your survival tin should include the following items:

- Matches. Use these only when other fire-making methods fail.
- Candle. This will give you a source of light and help you to start a fire. Candle wax can be also be eaten in an emergency.
- **Flint**. Make sure you have a flint with a saw striker. These can be used to make hundreds of fires, and will carry on working long after your matches have been used up.
- Sewing kit. This is useful for repairing clothes.
- Water purification tablets. These will help you have clean water to drink.
- Compass. A small button, liquid-filled compass is the best, but check it regularly for leaks.

This private from the Royal Australian Regiment, 1951, carries the British backpack and webbing.

- Mirrors. As they are reflective, they can be used for signaling.
- Safety pins. These are useful for securing items of clothing and for making fishing lines.
- Fish hooks and line. The fishing kit should also include split lead weights. Have as much line as possible—it can also be used to catch birds.
- Wire saw. This can cut even large trees (cover it in a film of grease to protect it against rust).
- Large plastic bag. This can be used to carry water and used as the lining for a **solar still** to make water.
- Snare wire. A brass wire is the best that can be used for animal traps.

Tents and shelters

If you are sleeping outdoors, you will obviously need a tent. There is a vast range of tents from which to choose. Most modern tents are not heavy, so go for a tent that has plenty of space inside. **Bivi-bag**s are another type of portable shelter. In reality, they are a waterproof overall for a sleeping bag. Some have

The contents of a survival tin, including flint and striker, sewing kit, candle, matches, compass, fishing equipment, and painkillers.

The wilderness usually has plenty of materials for constructing a shelter. Canada alone has 1.61 million square miles (2.5 million sq km) of forest land packed with usable trees.

hoops that make them into one-person tunnel tents. It is not really practical to cook inside a bivi-bag, because it is so confined, but it is windproof, waterproof, and very lightweight.

Cooking

The right cooking equipment is also important. There are lots of cooking stoves to choose from, but there are two very important rules you should bear in mind when making your choice:

- Keep it as lightweight as possible.
- Do not buy a stove that has a lot of delicate pieces—they can be easily snapped off and lost when being used in the outdoors.

You will need cookware and crockery to go with your stove and there is a large choice available. They usually come in sets of four or five items that fit inside one another to form a very compact set—excellent for space-saving. However, before you rush out and buy a set, ask yourself if you really need this amount of cooking pans. For crockery, you obviously want a set that is hard-wearing and light. Plastic is probably the best; it is tough and will not rust.

Mess tins are made of aluminum because the metal is very light, but it is also an excellent conductor of heat, so fluids boil quickly.

Food

So what food should you take with you into the wilderness? The backpacker should carry dehydrated food that is made for outdoor pursuits. This means that it will contain all the right ingredients to give you energy and keep you healthy. As a general rule, avoid cans: they are bulky and awkward to carry. There are many camping foods available that come in sealed packets. All you do is pour in hot water and stir, then wait for a couple of minutes, and you have a hot, nutritious meal. In addition, there are many survival ration packs that you can purchase. These tend to be compact packs that contain meals and can keep you going for 24 hours. Here is an example of the contents of a 24-hour ration pack issued to a British Army soldier.

• Breakfast—warm oatmeal, drinking chocolate.
• Snack—chicken spread, cookies (fruit and plain), chocolate, chocolate caramels, nuts and raisins, dextrose sweets.
• Main meal—vegetable soup, curried beef granules, rice, peas, apple, and apricot flakes.

Backpacks

Everything you take with you needs to be carried, so you will need a backpack. There are many backpacks available to the adventurer, large and small. However, remember to get a pack that is suited to your needs. If you get a 26-gallon (100-liter) pack when really you need only a 13-gallon (50-liter) one, you will probably end up filling the large pack to the brim and carry around too much weight.

Find a backpack that is comfortable and easy to use. Here are some of the things you should look for when buying a backpack:

• Side pockets, useful for carrying items that you need to get to quickly.

Kit including water bottle, rope, a mess tin, Swiss Army knife, and a compass. The backpack can weigh up to 100 pounds (45 kg).

- Base compartment, a good place for putting wet items so they do not soak the rest of your equipment.
- Double stitching to increase strength and protection.

Making a pack

There is also the horseshoe pack that can be used to carry items over long distances. Here's how to make one: lay a square-shaped material five feet by five feet (1.5 m x 1.5 m) on the ground (see below: A). Place all items on one side of the material and then roll the material with the items to the opposite edge. Tie each end and have at least two evenly spaced ties around the roll (B). Then bring both ends together

If you do not have a purpose-built backback, you can improvise one out of square sheet of material. Follow the steps above.

and secure. What you now have is a compact and comfortable pack, which you can change from shoulder to shoulder if required (C).

Sleeping bag

Finally, one essential piece of survival kit is the sleeping bag. Good sleeping bags are filled with "down," the best insulating material. In wet conditions, you will need a waterproof cover for a down-filled bag. If you know you will be sleeping in wet conditions, then you should get a bag filled with Holofil®. You could opt for an all-weather sleeping bag that is light but expensive. They consist of a sleeping bag, a fleece liner, and a bivi-bag.

If you are carrying all these items, then you do not really have to worry about survival. However, disaster can strike and the special forces soldier needs to know how to find food and water if he or she runs out of supplies.

SURVIVAL KNIVES

A knife is extremely important in a survival situation. It can be used for many things, such as skinning animals, preparing fruits and vegetables, and cutting trees. Always keep your knife clean and sharp and make sure it is securely fastened when you are traveling. There are many knives to choose from, but it is best to have one that has a single blade and a wooden handle. Never throw your knife into trees or into the ground because you could damage it or it could become lost.

WATER

Of all the elements of survival, water is the most important. Without water, there is no life. Therefore all Canadian and Australian soldiers must know where to find, and how to make, water if they are to live in the wild for any length of time.

In a survival situation, a person may be able to live without food for weeks in certain conditions. Without water, however, he or she will die within days. Therefore, finding water is the number-one priority for all survivors. In a temperate climate, a person needs to drink at least a half gallon (2.5 liters) of water a day. Even if you are doing very little physical activity, you need water to replace fluids lost. **Dehydration**—when you lose more water than you are drinking—is a life-threatening condition. The symptoms are a loss of appetite, lethargy, impatience, sleepiness, stress, slurred speech, and a failure to think straight. The treatment is straightforward: replace lost fluids by drinking water.

Because sweating and breathing too hard can make dehydration worse if the survivor does not have plenty of water, you should do the following:

• Keep all physical activity to a minimum.
• Perform all tasks slowly to save energy, and take regular rest periods.
• In hot climates, work at night or during the cooler parts of the day.

To make a flask of clean and safe water, this soldier is pouring it into his Pre-Mac PWP personal water purifier.

Marching during the day like these Canadian soldiers can be very tiring and should be done only if water supplies are plentiful.

- Keep clothing on to reduce fluid loss. There is a temptation to take off clothing in hot climates. Don't!
- Wear light-colored clothing in hot weather: it reflects the sun's rays and keeps you cooler.

Water bottles should be an essential item in any backpacker's kit. Plastic and **aluminum** models are available, though remember aluminum ones can be placed in a fire to heat the water if required.

If you do not have plenty of water with you, you will have to find natural sources of water. Luckily, wooded, hilly, or mountainous areas usually have many streams, freshwater lakes, or other water sources. The following signs are often an indication that water is close by:

- Swarming insects. Look out especially for bees and columns of ants.
- Birds. These may gather around water.
- Lots of plants of many different types. This often means that the plants are drinking from water that is near the surface.
- Animals. At dusk and dawn, many animals, especially those that eat grass, need water.

"Webbing" is the term used for the system of belts, straps, and pouches a soldier uses to hold his kit. The pouches here contain ammunition, a water bottle, and rations.

- Large clumps of lush grass.
- Springs and water seeping in rocky terrain.
- Cracks in rocks with bird dung outside. This may indicate a very small or narrow water source that can be reached by a straw.
- Valley floors. Dig along their sloping sides to find water.

Solar still

If you can find water, there are several ways of making it. A solar still is one of the best. Dig a hole three feet (90 cm) across and two feet (60 cm) deep. Dig a small hole in the middle of the bigger hole and put a container in it. Then place a plastic sheet over the hole

and hold it in place around the edges with sand, dirt, or rocks. Place a rock in the center of the sheet. When it gets hot, water vapor condenses on the underside of the plastic sheet and runs down into the container.

Transpiration bag

If you are in a wooded area, a transpiration bag is a very simple way of getting water.

A simple method of collecting rain water is to wrap a cloth around a slanted tree and ensure the bottom of the cloth drips into a container.

Green bamboo often contains trapped water. You can cut off the end section with a knife and drink from it.

Place a large plastic bag over the living limb of a tree or large shrub. The bag opening is sealed at the branch. The limb is then tied or weighted down so that water will flow to the corner of the bag. Of course, an even better way of getting water is by catching rain water. A simple method of collecting rain water is to wrap a cloth around a slanted tree and ensure the bottom of the cloth drips into a container.

Purifying water

When you have taken water from a stream or river, you will need to both filter it and purify it before you drink. Remember, filtering does not purify water, it only removes the solid particles like bits of soil. One way to filter the water is to pour it through a piece of cloth such as a cotton T-shirt. Do this a few times if possible. Then you have to purify it. This means that you kill any diseases or nasty infections

This improvised water catcher uses a leaf as a gutter. The rainwater is directed down the leaf and into a metal container beneath it.

that might lurk in the water. Soldiers of the Canadian and Australian Special Forces are taught these three simple ways of purifying water:

• Use water purification tablets. (Use one tablet if the water is clear water, two if it is cloudy.)
• Five drops of two percent iodine in a container of clear water; 10 drops in cloudy or cold water. (Let it stand 30 minutes before drinking.)
• Boil water for 10 minutes.

If you follow these procedures, then you should have plenty of water to keep you alive in the wilderness. If you are struggling to find water, however, reduce the amount you eat. The process of digesting food uses a lot of your body's water. If you cannot find any water at all, you are best not eating anything until you find a proper water source.

IDENTIFYING CONTAMINATED WATER

As well as purifying any water they find, elite forces soldiers are trained to identify poisonous water sources and avoid them. Look for the following signs that water is not healthy to drink:

• It smells bad.
• It has foam or bubbles on the surface.
• It has a strange color.
• It has no healthy plants growing around it.

FIRE

In the Canadian and Australian Special Forces, you must learn how to make fire from the natural materials around you. Fire is used not only as a heat source but also as a means of cooking food. Do not rely on matches to survive. This chapter explains how elite units make fires and keep them going.

Fire has long been one of the most important tools of human beings. From prehistoric times, humans learned how to create fire by creating friction with tools, such as saws and drills, and by producing sparks with stones such as flint. Whatever wilderness you find yourself in, a fire is always essential. A fire will provide warmth and dry clothes; it will cook food and heat drinks; it will keep wild animals at bay and ward off insects; it provides light; it can be used for signaling; and it provides a special morale booster.

In order to start and maintain a successful fire, it is vital to collect the right material and to get the balance right between the different elements of the fire, which are air, heat, and fuel.

The first material you need is **tinder**. This is required to get a fire started from the first sparks. Tinder can be wood shavings, thin strips of bark, sawdust, cotton fluff, bird down, dried grass, or pine straw. The next stage in fire-making is **kindling**. This is the material you use to really get the fire going so that you can put on

One thing soldiers will never be short of in the wilderness is wood, but they must have a flint or some other fire-making equipment.

The fire plough, one of the oldest methods of making fire, dates back to about 9,000–3,000 years B.C.

larger pieces of material to burn. It includes twigs, bark, tufts of dry grass, paper, or rags soaked in fuel. Finally, there is the fuel itself. This may be wood, such as dead branches or the inside of trees, coal, peat (as long as it is dry enough), dry animal manure, or dry grasses twisted into bunches.

Before you actually start your fire, you have to choose somewhere to build it. Build the fire in a place where it will not be put out by a strong wind or falling snow, or where it is likely to set light to vegetation or your equipment. The fire should be built on a firm base. This can be made up of stones, green wood, or solid earth. (This may involve digging down.) The fire may need to be in a hole in the ground or surrounded by rocks if wind is likely to be a problem. But there is one final point you should remember. Fires need air to burn. If you smother a fire with too many logs before it is going properly, you will snuff it out.

There are a number of different kinds of fires that are suitable for different uses and areas.

Safety night fire

This type of fire is designed to burn through the night with minimal risk of falling logs. It is designed to have few air spaces, so that the flame will burn low, and two leaning logs have the effect of pushing the fire away from your shelter.

Long fire

This fire can be made either as a trench or between two parallel green logs. The logs should be thick, and may be supported by two sticks to improve the airflow.

Teepee fire

This fire is good for both cooking and heat. It is made with a slanting stick fixed into the ground over some tinder.

The teepee fire is one of the best fires for air circulation.

Other sticks are then leaned on it, leaving a suitable opening on the wind side. The fire should be lit with your back to the wind.

T-fire

This is a fire kindled in a simple "T" shape carved out in the earth. It is an ideal fire for cooking on, since the main fire can be kept in the top part of the T, while cooking can be done on hot coals and embers that fall into the stem of the T.

Star fire

An economical fire that should be made with hardwood logs. The logs are arranged in a star shape and gradually pushed inward as they burn away.

Pyramid fire

Lay two logs parallel to each other, and lay a number of smaller logs across them to form a base. Lay another layer of yet smaller logs at right angles to form the next layer, and so on, until you have a small layer at the top on which to light your tinder. The fire will gradually burn downward, making it a good slow-burning fire to have during the night.

A pyramid fire is lit from the top, not the bottom. The fire will gradually burn downward, making it a good long-term fire to have throughout the night.

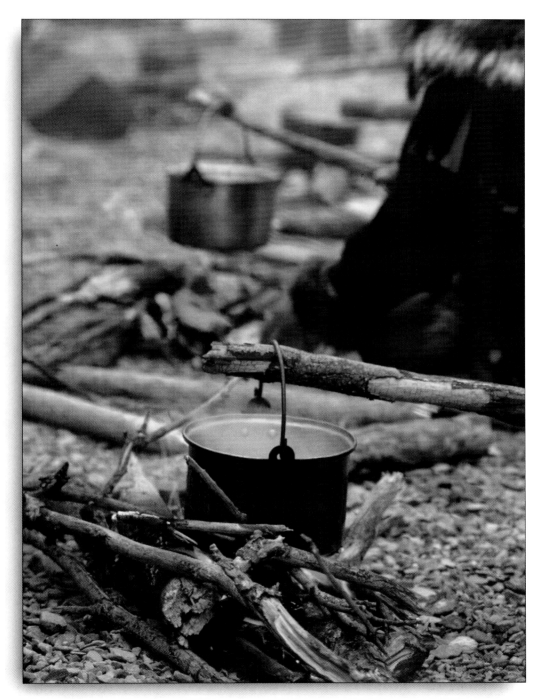

Metal containers become extremely hot when left over a fire. Use a stick to lift the container off the heat after cooking, never your hands.

When it actually comes to lighting a fire, make sure you gather all materials in front of you before you start. Windproof matches are the easiest and most obvious way of lighting a fire—you should have a set in your survival kit. You might, however, wish to keep these for emergencies or you may have run out. If you are planning to set out on a journey, make sure you have these matches, since you will have less time when traveling to set up other means of fire lighting.

A magnifying glass can be used to light a fire. Again, you should carry a magnifying glass in your survival kit. Its advantage over matches is that it will not wear out. Angle the glass so that the sun shines through it. Then move it backward and forward until you have a single spec of hot light. Concentrate this on to some dry tinder, which should start smoking and then glow red. Blow gently to make a flame.

In your survival kit, you should have a fire-lighting piece of equipment that consists of a small saw and a small metal bar—a flint. It is easy to draw the saw across the bar to produce a strong spark. Alternatively, strike a piece of flintstone with metal for the same effect.

The bow and drill

One of the oldest methods of making fire is the bow and drill. Make the bow from a piece of **willow** with a string stretched across it, end to end. The drill should be a single shaft of dry wood with one end pointed and the other rounded. The rounded end should fit into a hole hollowed out of a fist-sized piece of wood, which is used to hold the drill vertically in the hand. The pointed end goes downward into a notch in a piece of wood below that is tinder.

Twist the string around the shaft and move the bow in a regular way back and forth so that the string turns the drill. With increasing pressure and speed, it creates the friction in the lower block of wood that will eventually produce smoke and light the tinder. Then remove the bow and spindle and place the tinder next to the glowing ember. Roll tinder around the burning ember and blow to burn the tinder.

A hand drill is a similar method to the bow and drill, but without the bow. Rub a piece of hollow softwood between your hands, running them down the shaft as you go. The effect will be similar to that described above.

Fire will be a priority for any elite soldier making a base for the night. Of course, one of the best reasons for making a fire is for cooking. We'll look at the subject of food in the next chapter.

FIRE SAFETY

Follow these rules when making a fire to avoid getting hurt:
- Move anything that might explode well away from the fire. This includes wet stones that can blow apart if heated up.
- Do not make a fire in a shelter that has very little ventilation—the smoke will poison you.
- Clear away vegetation from around the fire—you do not want to start a forest fire.
- Make your fire in a place that you can easily escape from if the fire gets out of control.

FOOD

No matter where you are, there are many types of plant and animal foods available. Soldiers from the Canadian and Australian armies must learn where to find them, how to recognize them, how to collect or trap them, and be able to tell what is poisonous and dangerous.

Elite soldiers are taught many different types of cooking for the wild. Food can be boiled in a metal container, or in coconut shells, sea shells, turtle shells, and half sections of bamboo. Food can also be fried by putting a flat piece of rock on a fire; when it is hot, fry food on it. Baking takes a bit more hard work. Make an oven by digging a pit under a fire. Another method of baking is to line a pit with dry stones and build a fire in the pit. As the fire burns down, scrape the coals back and put your food container in. Then cover it with a layer of coals and a thin layer of dirt. The food will then bake. Roasting is easier, as it can be done with a skewer or spit over an open fire.

Plant food

So what food can you actually eat? Let's look at plants first. There are thousands of edible plants in the wild. The survivor should carefully examine the area he or she is in for edible plant species.

Once killed, an animal must be stripped of its fur or feathers before cooking. This soldier demonstrates how to pluck a chicken.

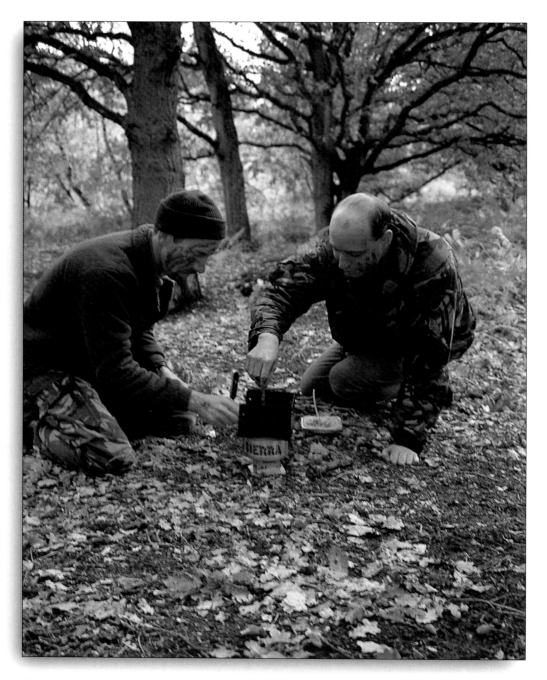

Food is vital for energy. Food energy is released in digestion, when the body breaks down the food into its elements and provides heat, rather like a furnace.

If you have to eat unknown plants, you must carry out the taste test to see if they are safe to eat (see page 59). It is important to test all parts of the plant—many plants have only one or more edible parts.

It is impossible here to list all the edible plants you will find in the wild. Use these simple Army guidelines, used by many forces around the world (including the U.S. Special Forces), to guide you as to whether something is safe or not.

- Umbrella-shaped flowers are generally poisonous. However, carrots, celery, and parsley are the exceptions to this rule.
- Beans and peas can make you feel sick and give you stomach ache or diarrhea.

The leaf stalks of the burdock plant can be eaten raw or cooked, and the roots boiled.

- Avoid all bulbs.
- All white and yellow berries are poisonous; half of all red berries are also poisonous.
- Blue or black berries are generally safe to eat.
- Single fruits on a stem are usually edible.
- A milky **sap** means that the plant is usually poisonous.
- Plants that make your skin itch when you touch them should not be eaten.
- Plants that grow in water are generally edible and often tasty.

Animal food

Plants are only one source of food. Animals are another. You must become good at hunting and trapping to use animals as a food source to survive. Learn about the types of animals that live in the area you are in, their tracks, habits, and where they sleep. All animals will provide you with meat of one kind or another. However, unless you have a gun, you will catch most animals with snares and traps. Most of what you will catch in this way will be small animals and birds.

If you do have a gun, bow and arrow, or spear, obey the following rules when hunting prey: Walk as quietly as possible. Move slowly and stop frequently to listen. Be observant. Blend in with the terrain features if you can. Be prepared; animals often startle the hunter and catch him off guard.

Mammals are probably the best food source for the survivor. They are divided into the following groups:

- Wild cats. These vary in size from small domestic cats to lions and tigers. Depending on the size of cat, you will either need a spring snare or a gun.
- Wild dogs. Although they can be caught with snares, wild dogs are best avoided because they have a nasty bite.
- Bears. They should only be tackled if you have a gun. They are large and strong creatures which can kill a person easily, so beware.
- Weasels, stoats, mink, martens, and polecats. All of these animals have sharp teeth and can give a nasty bite.

- Wolverines—badger-shaped animals. These should be tackled only if you have a gun.
- Badgers. These are an excellent food source that can be caught in spring snares and deadfall traps.
- Cattle. Large cattle, especially bulls, can be dangerous.
- Deer and antelopes. The small types can be caught in snares and deadfalls, and the larger ones by spear traps and larger deadfalls. But beware of their horns, as they can gorge and stab and inflict serious wounds.

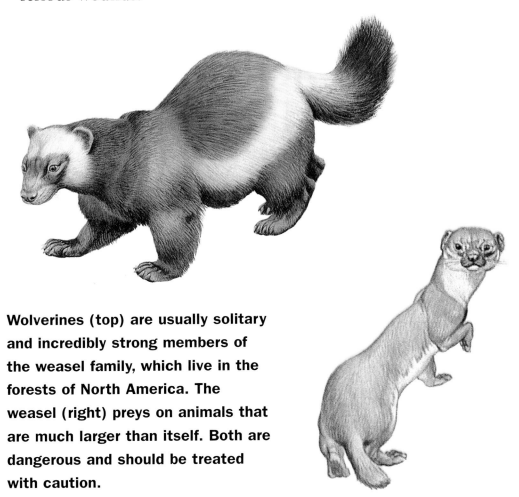

Wolverines (top) are usually solitary and incredibly strong members of the weasel family, which live in the forests of North America. The weasel (right) preys on animals that are much larger than itself. Both are dangerous and should be treated with caution.

- Wild pigs. Their tusks can cause serious injury. They can be caught with strong spring snares, deadfalls, and pig spear traps.
- Rodents and rabbits are plentiful and easily caught with snares.
- Reptiles. They can be a valuable food source, but some can be extremely dangerous. Reptiles that are best left alone: crocodiles, alligators, Gila monsters, and beaded lizards. Do not eat toads because they have toxic skin secretions.
- Snakes. Treat all snakes as dangerous and poisonous, even if they are not. Use a forked stick to pin them down just behind the head. Then club the back of the head with another stick. Better still, cut off the head with a machete. Never pick up a snake until you are sure it is dead.

  - Snails, worms, and slugs. Eat these only when they are fresh. Avoid snails with brightly colored shells because they are poisonous. Avoid sea snails in tropical waters, as some have stings that can kill. With worms, starve them for a day or squeeze them between the fingers to clear out their insides.

A female rabbit can produce up to 56 young each year, so they are always a plentiful food source in the wilderness.

Snares and traps

Of course, all these animals need to be caught before you can eat them. The main type of traps are snares, deadfall traps, and spear

As long as you have some rope in your kit, snares and traps can be made wherever there is wood.

traps. A snare is a wire or string loop placed in such a way that an animal is forced to put its head through it. The snare will then tighten, thus killing the animal (though sometimes not immediately). Deadfall traps are simple: when the bait is taken by the animal, a weight falls on the prey and kills it. There are many types of deadfall triggers—the bit of the traps that causes the weight to fall. Most are activated by a **tripwire** or when the animal knocks away a stick that is holding up the weight. Spear traps can be very effective. These are a springy shaft that is held in place by a tripline, with a spear tied to the springy shaft. This spear hits the animal when released. Warning: these traps can kill. Always approach them from behind.

You do not have to eat only animals on land. Special forces soldiers are also trained in survival fishing. There are fish in the seas, rivers, and lakes in all parts of the world, and they can be caught relatively easily. The hooks and lead weights in your survival kit are worth their weight in gold. Use the fishing methods listed here to catch fish using your line, weights, and hooks.

A fish basket is an ingenious and ancient method of fishing. The fish easily swims into the basket, but once it is inside, the sticks near the entrance make it hard to swim out.

Still fishing

Used for catching fish on the river bed. First, weight your line, then attach a baited hook and let it settle on the bottom of the river or float. You must then sit back and be patient. Remember to pull on the line at frequent intervals to check for a bite.

Dry fly fishing

Different from still fishing, this method is designed to catch fish that feed on the surface of the water. Dry fly fishing is only recommended in hot weather when airborne insects are plentiful; otherwise the fish will not bite. You can improvise a line with a stick and a length of string. Cast the **fly** upstream and let it float down past you. Then wait for the fish to bite.

Once animal food has been caught, it should be gutted and then it can be cooked using the cooking methods we have already looked at. With plant foods, this should give you plenty to eat in the wild.

TASTE TEST

Use this simple test for establishing whether a plant is safe to eat. It cannot be applied to fungi—many are deadly, so do not eat any of them.

- Choose a small portion of the plant.
- Test only one part of the plant at a time.
- Break the plant into its different parts: leaves, stem, and roots.
- Smell the plant for unpleasant odors.
- Do not eat for eight hours before starting the test.
- During this period, put a piece of the plant on the inside of your elbow or wrist. Wait for 15 minutes to see if you develop a rash or burning sensation.
- During the test, do not eat anything (except the plant) and drink only pure water.
- Touch it on the outer part of your lip to test for burning or itching.
- If there is no reaction after three minutes, place it on your tongue; hold for 15 minutes.
- If there is no reaction, chew a piece thoroughly and hold it in your mouth for 15 minutes. Do not swallow.
- If there is no irritation whatsoever during this time, swallow the food.
- Wait eight hours. If you feel ill, make yourself vomit (stick two fingers down your throat) and drink plenty of water.

SHELTER

In a survival situation you must find shelter or build your own to protect you from the wind, cold, and wet. Learn from the Canadian and Australian Special Forces how to construct your wilderness shelter in the right place and from the proper materials.

There are several general points about shelters which you should bear in mind when you are in a survival situation in the wilderness. Of course, if you are suddenly trapped by the weather, or are injured or exhausted, almost any natural shelter will do. For example, get into a hollow in the ground and add to its height by piling up rocks around it.

There is a temptation if you are in a warm and dry climate to assume that you will need less shelter, even no shelter at all. However, remember that whatever the temperature during the day, at night it will get cold. Many warm areas can become incredibly chilly at night. In addition, a shelter can provide protection against dangers and wildlife. Snakes, for example, are attracted to body warmth and have been known to crawl into the sleeping bags of backpackers lying in the open and curl themselves up next to the sleeping person. Therefore, do not believe that you can do without shelter in the wild.

Do not build your shelter just anywhere. Make sure the ground is level; check for insects and for overhead branches that may fall on you.

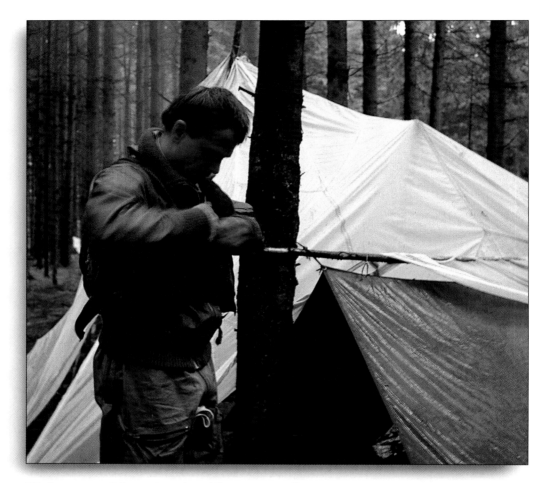

Make use of tree trunks. They are a firm base to which you can lash your shelter and ensure it does not blow over in strong winds.

Choosing the right site for a shelter is very important. If you select a bad site, you will probably end up building another shelter in a better spot, and will thus waste valuable time and energy. Do not select a site in the late afternoon after a long day's walk or march. You will be tired and in no mood to make a good choice. Your decision will invariably be a bad choice and may force you into using poor materials.

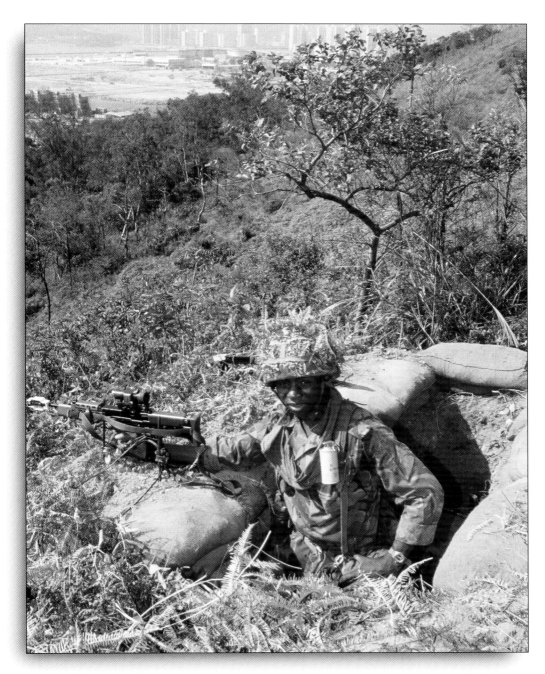

Underground shelters are much cooler than shelters on top of the earth. This is because the soil stops the sun's rays, and also acts as a reservoir for storing cool water.

Soldiers surviving behind enemy lines use the natural foliage of the wilderness to conceal their equipment from enemy troops.

The weather can also play a key part in what shelter you build and where you build it. In warm areas, build shelters in areas to take advantage of breezes, but beware of exposing a shelter to blowing sand or dust, both of which can cause injury and damage. In cold regions, choose a site that is protected from the effects of wind and

MOVING BETWEEN CAMPS

When shifting from one camp to another, keep your load as light as possible and distribute the weight evenly; put all the most important items within easy access, particularly the tools you will need to build the next camp; put everything in plastic bags to protect against water; and take with you only what you need.

drifting snow. Rain, sleet, and snow can all be potential hazards. Do not build a shelter where water runs, in a site that is prone to flash floods or mud slides, nor in an avalanche area.

Insects can be a problem around a camp. If you build your shelter where there is a breeze or steady wind, you can reduce the number of insects that will pester you. Avoid building a shelter near ponds or lakes, as it attracts mosquitoes, bees, wasps, and hornets. Do not build a shelter on or near an ant hill, unless you want lots of bites and stings!

The type of shelter you build depends on the conditions and the materials available. Remember, it is often a good idea to make a temporary shelter to give you some form of protection from the elements until you can erect something more permanent (particularly if it is getting dark and cold).

If you cannot find any materials, make use of natural shelters. In open areas, sit with your back to the wind and pile up equipment behind you as a windbreak. The following are all examples of natural shelters that the survivor can use in an emergency situation:

- Brambles and boughs that sweep down to the ground or are partly broken. Add branches to make them more dense.
- Natural hollows provide protection from the wind. Use a few strong branches, covered with sticks and turf, as a roof.
- Fallen tree trunks. Scoop out a hollow on the sheltered side and cover with boughs to make a roof.
- Stones or small rocks can be used to increase the height of your hollow. To insulate against the wind, plug the gaps with turf and foliage mixed with mud.

- Caves can make excellent shelters. If it is in a cliff or mountain, increase your cave's warmth by building a windbreak over the entrance.

You can use stones, rocks, or turf cut like bricks. If you intend to light a fire in a cave, remember to light it at the back—smoke from a fire at the front of a cave will circulate against the air current and will choke you!

A hammock, made from a poncho, can be tied between two or more trees for greater stability.

WHERE NOT TO BUILD A SHELTER

Elite forces soldiers often have to build shelters quickly when on operations behind enemy lines. They know they must avoid the following spots:

• On a hilltop exposed to wind: it will be cold and windy.

• In a valley bottom or deep hollow: they could be damp and frosty at night.

• On pieces of land that lead to water: they are often routes to animals' watering places.

• Below a tree containing a bees' or hornets' nest or dead wood. Dead wood could come crashing down on you in the next high wind.

• Under a solitary tree: it can attract lightning.

There are, of course, an almost limitless variety of shelters you can build in the wild. Use your imagination, but do not forget the basic principles. Elite soldiers are taught to build shelters that give:

• Protection from the cold.
• Protection from the snow.
• Protection from the wind.
• Protection from the damp.
• Protection from insects.
• Protection from too much sun.

IMPROVISING TOOLS AND WEAPONS

The elite forces soldier is trained to make provisions including tools, weapons, and clothing, from the raw materials he or she finds in the wilderness. If carefully made, these can work better than manufactured alternatives, so practice is the key.

Being able to fashion tools from the materials you find will make your task of staying alive that much easier. It will also act as a great confidence booster. For instance, if you are stranded in the wilderness with only one knife and it breaks, it could be a disaster. However, if you are able to make an alternative, perhaps from wood or metal, your disappointment will be shortlived. In a survival situation, the number of things you can improvise is limited only by your imagination.

Club

A club has a variety of uses for the survivor. It can be used for checking snares and traps (you must not use your hands because you may get injured), killing a trapped animal, and as a weapon.

A club is extremely simple to make—so much so that if it breaks it can be replaced very easily. So whether you are in mountains or desert climates, a club will be the most useful tool you can make. All

Troops use a wire-cutting tool to trim wire for building shelters. If troops do not have a manufactured tool, they must improvise.

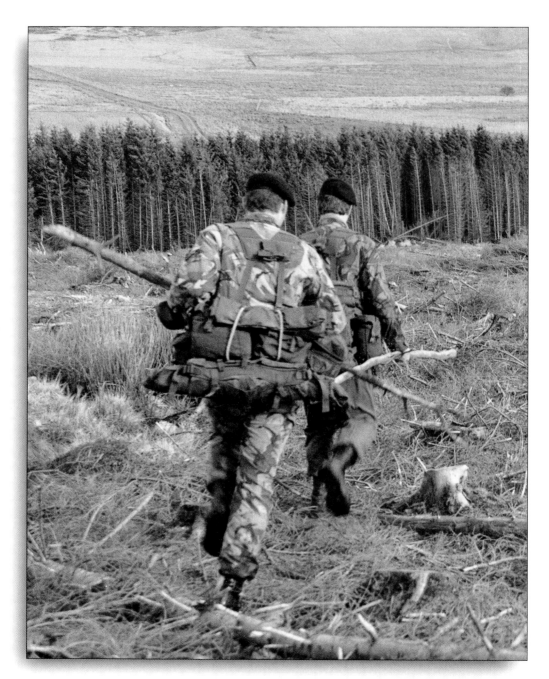

Soldiers cut down sections of pine for making shelters. Pine is a very useful tree, producing oils, tars, charcoal, and edible pine nuts, as well as a strong wood.

Stone and wood tools were first produced in prehistoric times. Hand axes were used in Africa and Asia about one million years ago.

you need is a tree branch about two to two and a half inches (5–6 cm) in diameter and around two and a half feet (75 cm) long.

Stone tools

Although wood is probably the most plentiful natural resource for the survivor, stones and rocks are also readily available. Flint, **obsidian**, and quartz make good hammers. Either use them on their own or tie them to a handle.

Bone tools

The bones of any large animal can be used to make tools, so if you have snared or clubbed an animal for food, do not throw away the carcass. With improvisation, the antlers and horns of reindeer can be made into a makeshift spade which you can use to dig for food and water, or a hammer for building a shelter. You can even make a saw for cutting wood from discarded animal bones—a shoulder blade split in half with teeth cut along it will fit this purpose. Finally, the ribs from small animals can be sharpened into points and used as miniature spears or arrows.

Bow and arrows

The bow and arrow has been used for centuries as a hunting tool all around the world. In the United States, Native American tribes

Hunting bows come in many different sizes. Some bows in ancient Japan are an astonishing eight feet (2.4 m) long, about three feet (90 cm) longer than the typical user at the time.

Improvised knifes can be made from wood, bone, stone, or metal.

such as the Apaches, Comanches, and Sioux used them to kill buffalo and other migrating animals for hundreds of years before and after Columbus discovered the "New World" in 1492.

Above all, a bow must be springy. Yew is the best wood for this, but you may have to use other wood if yew does not grow where you are. The bow should be about four feet (1.2 m) long. It must be two inches (5 cm) wide at the center and a half inch (1.5 cm) wide at the ends, where the wood should be notched to take the string. The arrows should be made from smooth and straight wood that is two feet (60 cm) long and a quarter inch (6 mm) wide. You should notch one end a quarter inch (6 mm) deep to fit the string of the bow. A variety of materials can be used to make flights, including paper, feathers, or leaves. Arrow heads can be made of tin, flint, bone, or the wood burned black. You must put a notch in the end of each arrow to fit over your bowstring.

To shoot, first place an arrow in the bowstring. Then raise the center of the bow to eye-level. Hold the bow in the center with your left hand (if you are right-handed) and rest the arrow on top of it. This arm should remain locked as you pull back the bowstring with your other hand. You must line up the target with the arrow and then release the string, making sure you do not snatch at it as you release. Always make sure you have several arrows, in case you miss your target first time.

Spears

Besides a club, a spear is the next most useful tool for killing game, and they can also be used to trap fish. A stick with a sharpened point is the simplest form of spear, but this can break quite easily. A more durable spear will feature specially built heads. In the wilderness, you can use animal bone, flint, or tin for this purpose. They are lashed to the handle of the spear with string.

The machete is essential kit for the wilderness. "Machete" is a Spanish word, but other countries have different names for it, such as "golok," "parang," and "bolo."

Fish hooks and lines

Improvise fish hooks from pins, a bunch of thorns, nails, bones, or wood. You can make a fish snare to trap large fish such as pike, which often feed alongside weeds.

Catapult

Select a strong Y-shaped branch and a piece of elastic material. Make a pouch for the center of the elastic and thread it into position. Tie the ends of each side of the branch. Use stones or small rocks as missiles; with practice, you can become very accurate. With a sling shot, swing the sling above your head and release one end of the thong to send the ammunition in the direction of the target. When you are using a catapult against birds, use several stones at once.

MAKING A METAL KNIFE

A knife is a vital tool to have if you are a survivor. You can make one by following these steps:

- Find a piece of soft iron with a shape that resembles a knife blade.
- Place the metal on a flat, hard surface and hammer it to get the shape you desire.
- Rub the metal on a rough-textured rock to get a cutting edge and point.
- Tie the knife onto a hardwood handle.

RESCUE

Though an elite forces soldier can survive for a long time in the wilderness, he or she must eventually be rescued. Here we find out the best ways of attracting professional rescuers to you in the wilderness.

As a survivor, it is important that you are able to give signals that a rescue team, especially an aircraft, will be able to see clearly. You must plan how you are going to be rescued and be ready to put your plan into action quickly—a rescue airplane could appear at any moment and you may not get a second chance. Unless you have a radio or flares, smoke and fire are your best ways to alert a rescue aircraft. Three fires or three columns of smoke are recognized around the world as calls for help.

If you have come down in an aircraft or are in a life raft, you may have one or more professionally made signaling tools. If you are a backpacker, you are strongly advised to equip yourself with some of the items listed below:

- Radio. Survival radios work best when you are operating in clear, open terrain.
- Hand-held flares. Day flares make a bright-colored smoke; night flares are very bright and can be seen over long distances.

A Canadian soldier is winched aboard a Sea King helicopter during a simulated rescue mission in 1997.

Military radios come in many different forms. Some combat radios have a range of only about 25 miles (40 km), whereas some satellite phones can reach around the world.

- Hand-held launched flares. These are fired up into the air and can be seen from a long way away.
- Whistle. This is useful for short-range signaling.
- Light signals. Flashlights or strobe lights can be seen over great distances.
- Signal mirror. A mirror flash can be visible up to a range of 100 miles (160 km) in ideal conditions. On a sunny day, mirrors, polished canteen cups, belt buckles, or other objects will reflect the sun's rays.

Smoke signals

Smoke is one of your best tools to being found. In daylight, smoke will be seen over long distances. Try to create smoke that will contrast with the environment. If you put green leaves, moss, or damp wood on a fire, you will get white smoke; rubber or oil-soaked rags on a fire will produce black smoke. At night, bright fires are better for being seen. Build a fire on a high point, or even set fire to a tree. But be careful that your fires do not get out of control.

Ground-to-air signals

Ground-to-air signals are another good method of attracting attention from the air. There are several factors you must take into account. Above all, you must try to visualize what your signal will look like when viewed by a pilot from the air. The diagram (page 80) shows the internationally recognized emergency signals. Learn them, or better still carry a piece of paper around with you that lists them. When laying them out, make them as large as possible, at least 40 feet (10 m) long and 10 feet (3 m) wide. At night, dig or scrape a signal in the earth, snow, or sand, then pour in gasoline and ignite it. This signal will be visible not only at night, but also during the day where the ground has been burned. You must destroy all ground-to-air symbols after rescue; otherwise they will go on marking after you have gone. Failure to do so may result in other aircraft spotting them and attempting a rescue.

Once the rescue services know where you are, a rescue operation will be launched. On land, this will usually be in the form of a helicopter. Helicopters will make a rescue by landing or hovering. If a helicopter has to land to pick you up, do not approach it from the rear. It is a blind spot for the crew and the tail rotor is unprotected—it will kill you if it hits you. Also, be careful of being hit by the **rotors** if you are approaching the helicopter down a slope. Be aware of any materials on the ground that may be sucked into the rotor blades, such as a parachute or tent. Pick them up before the helicopter lands, including any leaves and twigs.

Try to mark the landing site with a large "H" at least 10 feet (3 m) high. However you make it, remember to make sure the materials are securely anchored to the ground so they do not fly up when the helicopter lands. If you are in sandy terrain, try to water the sand to keep dust down. In snow, try to press down the surface as much as possible. (Soft, wet snow will cling to the aircraft, and powdery snow will swirl and restrict the pilot's vision.)

If you are being winched aboard a hovering helicopter, let the cable touch

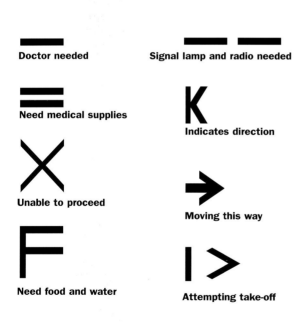

Doctor needed

Signal lamp and radio needed

Need medical supplies

K
Indicates direction

X
Unable to proceed

→
Moving this way

F
Need food and water

I>
Attempting take-off

Some of the internationally recognized ground-to-air signals used when trying to attract rescue.

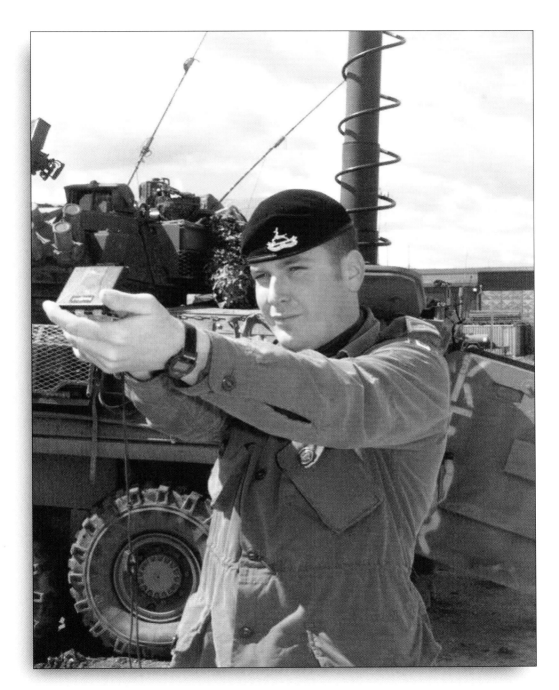

The compass used by this Canadian soldier is his main personal navigation instrument. Compasses were used in China by about A.D. 1100 and in Europe from 1187.

the ground before your touch it. (All aircraft build up a lot of **static electricity**, and you will receive a shock if you grab it before it discharges into the ground.) Fit yourself into the harness and then give the "thumbs up" sign. Do not make any further signals, especially raising your arms—you could slip out of the harness.

When you get to the cabin door, let the **winchman** do everything and obey everything he says. When you are out of the winch, you will be told to sit down and shown where to sit. Go

Australian soldiers on an airborne operation. Some military helicopters can lift up to 37,700 pounds (17,100 kg) of loads, so rescuing a team of survivors is no problem for them.

immediately to this place to be fastened into the seat. Remember to obey the aircrew at all times. Be careful when you leave the helicopter after it has touched down; wait for the rotors to stop turning—obey crew members at all times.

Once you are rescued, your survival situation is at an end. Helicopter and other rescue crews are called out to thousands of rescues each year. Most could have been avoided if the people had approached their outdoor adventure sensibly. Remember, you should be trained in survival, but you should never have to use your skills!

SIGNALS USING NATURAL MATERIALS

When you are stranded in the wild, construct signals from the materials around you.

- Build brush or snow mounds that will cast shadows.
- In snow, trample down the snow to form letters or symbols and fill in the spaces with contrasting materials such as twigs or branches.
- In sand, use boulders, vegetation, or seaweed to form a symbol.
- In brush-covered areas, cut out patterns in the vegetation.
- In tundra, dig trenches or turn the soil upside down.
- In any terrain, use contrasting materials so that the symbols are visible to aircraft.

DANGERS

If you get ill in the wilderness, your chances of survival are not good. If you act fast, and use elite forces training, the chances of coming through are much, much better.

The wilderness regions are full of dangers that the elite soldier must face with courage and skill. The main dangers are cold and heat. You must get out of the elements straight away and build a shelter. Otherwise you could find yourself falling victim to a wide range of illnesses, including dehydration, **hypothermia**, **frostbite**, sunburn, and **trench foot**.

Trench foot is an injury many elite soldiers had to fight in the Falklands War. It is caused by the feet being constantly cold and wet. In the early stages, feet and toes appear pale and feel numb, cold, and stiff. Walking is difficult and the feet swell and become painful. You must be alert to prevent trench foot: it can lead to **amputation**. To prevent trench foot, make sure you clean and dry your socks and boots regularly, and dry your feet as quickly as possible if they get wet. If wearing wet boots and socks, exercise your feet continually by wriggling your toes and bending your ankles. When treating trench foot, handle the feet very gently. Do not rub or massage them. Clean carefully with soap and water, dry, and then raise them up. Do not walk if you have trench foot.

A soldier from the Australian SAS regiment diffuses a mine in the Australian outback during Exercise "Tandem Thrust."

In the wilderness, you are also vulnerable to various illnesses carried by insects. You must try to prevent these illnesses through keeping clean. Try not to get cuts and scratches: in the wilderness, they can become infected very easily. Clean all cooking and eating utensils, dispose of garbage and human wastes, and protect food and utensils from flies. Do not expose your skin to the weather or to flies. Try to wash your feet and body daily. Change your socks regularly. You must check yourself for signs of any injury, and cover up any wounds with an adhesive bandage.

Animals are another danger. Bears are present in the northern forests and wastes. Steer clear of them: they are powerful and dangerous and can be killers, particularly when they have young.

Brown bears can grow a massive eight feet (2.4 m) long and run at an incredible 30 miles per hour (48 km/h) over short distances.

POISONOUS PLANTS

There are certain plants that the elite soldiers know not to eat in the wilderness. Find a good plant book and learn to identify all the plants listed below.

Plant	Effect
Poison sumac	Irritates skin
Poison ivy	Skin irritation and rash
Thorn-apple	Can kill if swallowed
Foxglove	Attacks the heart and can lead to death if eaten
Hemlock	Will create severe illness if eaten
Water hemlock/Cowbane	Lethal even if only one mouthful is ingested
Deadly nightshade	All parts of the plant are potentially lethal

Bears are powerful and tireless creatures that can pursue you for miles. Do not leave food scattered around your camp, as this will attract bears to you. Under no circumstances try to feed bears. Wild pigs have an aggressive nature and should be treated with caution. Some small pigs travel in groups of between 5 and 15, and in these numbers they can easily overcome a human. It is best to try to kill them at a distance with a spear. Do not try to tackle them yourself: their tusks can inflict severe injuries to your legs.

Even more than these larger animals, insects perhaps create the greater problems in wilderness survival. There are several types of dangerous or unpleasant insects and spiders that you will need to avoid in the wilderness.

Bees are often found collecting pollen from brightly colored flowers; do not disturb them.

Ants

Red ants live in pinewoods where they build nests as giant mounds. They live in groups of thousands and will bite viciously if they are disturbed.

Centipedes

There are some 3,000 species of centipede. They are carnivorous and feed mainly on a diet of worms. Mostly they are harmless, but some of the larger varieties will bite.

Hornets, bees, and wasps

All of these insects give off painful stings, which in some cases can be fatal. It is important that you check for nesting sites before building a shelter. In particular, wasps attack moving targets, so either remain still or hide in dense undergrowth where it will be difficult for the swarm to find you.

Scorpions

These are common in hot regions all over the world. Scorpions are characterized by two crablike pincers either side of the head, which are used to trap prey, and a poisonous spike in the tail.

Black widow spider

This is dangerously poisonous. Its bite can cause the human heart to stop in some cases.

Funnelweb spider

This is deadly poisonous. Found in Australia, it is small and black with short legs.

Ticks

Common in the tropics, ticks feed on blood. They have very powerful jaws for such small insects, which become embedded in the skin. To remove, expose them to heat, gasoline, or alcohol. Never pull them off.

With all insects, the soldiers of the Canadian and Australian Special Forces follow a set of rules that protect them from getting bitten. Remember the following tips when surviving in the wilderness: use insect repellent on exposed areas of skin; always wear clothing, especially at night when insects are more prevalent; wear gloves and a head net; camp well away from swamps; sleep under mosquito netting if you have it, or smear mud on your face to keep the insects away.

GLOSSARY

Amputation To remove or cut off a limb that has become infected to prevent infection spreading to other parts of the body.

Aluminum A very light and very strong metal often used to make survival equipment.

Bivi-Bag A special waterproof bag that can act like a mini tent. It is especially good for survival situations where there is not enough room to carry a full size tent.

Dehydrated food Food that has had the water content taken out. Dehydrated food is totally dry and lasts for a long time. Simply pouring cold or hot water onto it turns it back into normal food.

Dehydration An illness that occurs when someone loses more of their body's water than they take in through drink.

Flint A hard, gray rock that produces a shower of sparks when struck with a piece of metal. It is excellent for starting fires.

Fly In fishing, a fly is an object made to resemble an insect. It is put on the end of a fishing hoof to deceive fish into taking a bite.

Frostbite The name for a condition where parts of the body freeze in extreme cold, usually the fingers, toes, nose, ears.

Gore-Tex® A waterproof material that actually lets sweat pass through it into the air, but which will not let water droplets in.

Hypothermia A serious medical condition in which the victim's body temperature falls below a certain level.

Kindling Small pieces of burnable material—such as twigs and leaves—that are used to get a fire burning.

Obsidian A hard volcanic rock that has a very dark color.

Rotors The blades of a helicopter that enable it to fly.

Sap The fluid that flows inside of a plant or tree.

SAS The abbreviation of Special Air Service. The SAS is one of the world's most elite fighting forces and is the most expert regiment of the British Army.

Solar Still A method of making water using a plastic sheet.

Static electricity Electricity that is built up by friction. If it builds up enough, it can give someone a mild electric shock when they touch metal or any other material that conducts electricity.

Thermal clothing Special clothing that is designed to keep body heat in. Thermal clothing is recommended for those going into cold climates.

Tinder Tiny pieces of material, such as grass or sawdust, that ignite very easily and can be used to get a fire started.

Tripwire A piece of hidden wire that releases a trap or weapon when touched.

Trench foot A serious condition in which the feet become swollen and rotten from spending too long being wet and in boots.

Viet Cong The communist troops of South Vietnam who fought against the United States and South Vietnamese soldiers during the Vietnam War.

Vietnam War A war between North and South Vietnam in which the United States was involved between 1963 and 1973.

Willow A tree or shrub that has very "springy" branches, ideal for making bows and arrows or improvised fishing lines.

Winchman The person who works at the door of a helicopter and helps to winch people to safety during rescues.

EQUIPMENT REQUIREMENTS

Headwear
Safety helmet
Balaclava helmet
Woolen/thermal hat
Face protector

Clothing
Waterproof/windproof outer jacket
Thermal underjacket/fleece
Waterproof pants
Thermal underclothes
Many pairs of socks
Snow goggles

Footwear
Walking boots
Gaiters
Spare laces
Crampons
Skis
Snowshoes
Climbing boots (different boots are needed for different environments, so check before you go)

Load-carrying equipment
Backpack
Small carry sack
(All must be waterproof)

Survival equipment
Climbing rope
Walking rope

Carabiners (metal clips to which ropes can be attached)
Climbing anchors
Ice axe
Medical pack
Mess pack and knife/fork/spoon
Water bottle and mug
Survival knife
Lockable/retractable knife
Tent
Climbing and walking ropes
Sleeping bag
Plastic sheeting (to build shelters/make solar stills)
Sleeping mat
Survival bag
Telescopic walking stick or ski stick
Shovel/spade (foldable)
Compass
Watch
Chronograph
Flares
Signaling mirror (heliograph)
Binoculars
Map case
Wash pack
Matches
Flint and steel firelighter
Snare wire
Water purification tablets
Whistle
Candle (some candles are made to be edible)

CHRONOLOGY

July 1, 1942	The First Canadian Parachute Battalion is formed.
July 10, 1942	The Canadian Special Service Force is formed.
June 6, 1944	The Canadian paras go into action during D-Day, the Allied invasion of occupied Europe.
December 5, 1944	The Canadian Special Service Force is disbanded.
1947	The Canadian Special Air Service is formed, but disbanded in 1949.
1957	An Australian SAS unit is formed.
September 4, 1964	The Australian SAS expands to become the Australian Special Air Service Regiment.
1966	The Australian SAS is sent into the war in Vietnam.
April 8, 1968	The Canadian Airborne Regiment is created.
1971	After many hard years of fighting, the Australian SAS withdraws from Vietnam.
1974	The Canadian Airborne Regiment goes on its first peacekeeping operation.
April 1977	The Canadian Special Service Force is re-created.
1980s	The Australian SAS is put on alert three times after terrorist attacks or threats.
1991	The Canadian Airborne Regiment conducts a peacekeeping operation in the Western Sahara, Africa.
1995	Canadian Special Forces troops are deployed to Bosnia after Canadian soldiers are taken hostage.
1998	Australian SAS soldiers are sent to the Gulf in case of another outbreak of war with Saddam Hussein.
1999–2001	The Australian SAS conduct undercover missions to support Australian peacekeeping on the Pacific island of East Timor.

RECRUITMENT INFORMATION

Canadian Special Forces

To be eligible for the Canadian Army, you must:

- Be a Canadian citizen
- Be a minimum of 16 years old
- Have successfully completed Grade 10—Secondary III exams in Quebec
- Be clear of any judicial obligations for a period of at least 6 months prior to enrolment

Once in the Canadian Army, you can apply for Special Forces selection. For more information on joining the Canadian Army visit the following websites: http://www.army.dnd.ca/LF/home/index_e.html

http://www.cdnarmy.ca

http://www.dnd.ca

http://www.mapleleafup.org

http://home.crosswinds.net/cfarmy

Australian SAS

Entry into the Australian SAS is every bit as tough as its British equivalent. Like the British SAS, you need to be a regular soldier first. To join the Australian Army, you need to be an Australian citizen between 17 and 35 years of age. You have to go through a series of interviews and medical and intelligence tests before being assigned to an appropriate selection course. You will also have to do a fitness test. Like the other armies described here, there are many types of job in the Australian Army.

For information on the Australian Army, check out the the following websites:

http://www.army.gov.au

http://www.armyjobs.defence.gov.au

http://www.101.net.au

http://www.omen.net.au/eaglem/rae

http://iol.com.au/conway/ww1/army.html

FURTHER READING

Angier, Bradford and Vena Angier. *How to Stay Alive in the Woods.* Columbus, Ohio: Fireside, 1998.

Davenport, Gregory J. *Wilderness Survival.* Mechanisburg, Pa.: Stackpole Books, 1998.

Fears, Wayne. *The Complete Book of Outdoor Survival.* St. Iola, Wis.: Krause Publications, 2000.

Harvey, Mark. *The National Outdoor Leadership School's Wilderness Guide*: *The Classic Handbook.* Columbus, Ohio: Fireside, 1999.

Isaac, Jeffrey. *The Outward Bound Wilderness First-Aid Handbook.* New York: The Lyons Press, 1998

Montgomery, David. *Mountainman Crafts and Skills: A Fully Illustrated Guide to Wilderness Living and Survival.* New York: Lyons Press, 2000.

Springer, Joseph A. *The Black Devil Brigade: The True Story of the First Special Service Force in World War II.* Pacifica, Calif.: Pacifica Press, 2001.

Stillwell, Alexander. *The Encyclopedia of Survival Techniques.* New York: The Lyons Press, 2000.

Wiseman, John. *The SAS Survival Handbook.* New York: HarperCollins, 2001.

ABOUT THE AUTHOR

Dr. Chris McNab has written and edited numerous books on military history and elite forces survival. His publications to date include *German Paratroopers of World War II*, *The Illustrated History of the Vietnam War*, *First Aid Survival Manual*, and *Special Forces Endurance Techniques*, as well as many articles and features in other works. Forthcoming publications include books on the SAS, while Chris's wider research interests lie in literature and ancient history. Chris lives in South Wales, U.K.

INDEX

References in italics refer to illustrations

animals
  carcasses, to make
  tools 71–72
  dangerous 10, 86–87
  as food 50, 54–58
  as sign of water 37
  trapping 27
  see also insects
ants 88
arms *see* weapons

backpacks *25, 26,* 30–33, 92
bamboo, water from *39*
battles *see* fighting
bears 86–87
bees 88
bergens *see* backpacks
birds, as sign of water 37, 38
Bivi-bags 27–28
bone tools 71–72
boots *16,* 19–21
Borneo, Australian SAS in 11
Bosnia *14*
bow and arrows 72–74
bow and drill 48–49

camouflage *11, 15*
  Disruptive Pattern
  material (DPM) *18*
  Tiger Stripe Pattern *11*
camp sites 65
catapults 75
caves, for shelter 66
centipedes 88
chronology 93
cleanliness 86
clothing 16–23, 36, 92
  repairing 26
  uniforms *11,* 12
clubs 69–71
compasses 26, *31, 81*
conflict *see* fighting
contaminated water 41
cooking 28–29, *47*

dangers
  animals 10, 86–87
  illness 85–86
  insects 88–89
  poisonous plants 87
deadfall traps 57
dehydration 35–36
Disruptive Pattern Material
(DPM) camouflage *18*
dry fly fishing 58

equipment 24–33, 92

fighting
  Borneo 11

Vietnam War *8,* 11–12
World War II 10, 13
filtering water 39–41
fires 26, 42–49
first aid 10
  painkillers 27
  trench foot 85
fishing 58
  equipment 27, 75
flares 77, 78
flashlights 78
fleeces 19
FN FAL rifles *8*
food 10
  animals as *50,* 54–58
  cooking 28–29, *47*
  dehydrated food 25, 30
  plants as 51–53, 59
footwear 92
  boots *16,* 19–21
  socks 20, 21, 86
fuel, for fires 43–44

glossary 90–91
gloves 21–22
ground-to-air signals 79, *80*
guns *see* weapons

hammocks *66*
hand-held flares 77, 78
headwear 92
  hats 21–22
  insulating hats 16
helicopters
  rescue by 80–83
  Sea King helicopters *76*
history of the
  regiments 8–15
  chronology 93
hornets 88
horseshoe packs 32–33
hygiene 86

illness *see* first aid
insects
  carrying illness 86
  dangerous 88–89
  and shelters 65
  as sign of water 37
Internet addresses 94

jackets *16,* 19, 21

knives 33, *73,* 75

layer principle 19
light signals 78
lighting a fire 26, 48–49
list of equipment 92
long fires 45

M16 rifles *15*
machetes *74*
magnifying glasses 48
marching *36*
medicine *see* first aid
mirrors, for signaling 27, 78
moving between camps 65

natural materials for
signaling 83
natural shelters 61, 65–66
navigation 26, *31, 81*

pants 21
plants
  as food 51–53, 59
  poisonous 87
  as sign of water 37
  water from *39*
Pre-Mac PWP personal
water purifiers 34
purifying water *34,* 39–41
pyramid fires 46

radios 77, *78*
ration packs 30
recruitment information 94
rescue 76–83
rifles
  FN FAL rifles *8*
  M16 rifles *15*

safety night fires 45
scorpions 89
Sea King helicopters *76*
shelters 10, 27–28, 60–67, *70*
shirts 19
signaling 77–79
  mirrors 27
sleeping bags 33
smoke signals 79
snakes 56, 61
snares 56–57
snare wire 27
socks 20, 21, 86
solar stills 27, 38
spears 74
spear traps 57
spiders 89
star fires 46
still fishing 58
stone tools 71
survival tins 25–27
sweaters 19

"Tandem Thrust" exercise *84*
taste test 53, 59
teepee fires 45
tents 27–28

terrorism, Australian SAS 12
T-fires 45–46
thermal underwear 19
ticks 89
"Tiger Stripe"
camouflage pattern *11*
tools 68–75
  knives 33, *73,* 75
  snare wire 27
  wire saws 27
torches 78
training 6
  survival skills 9, 13
  "Tandem Thrust"
  exercise 84
transpiration bags 38–39
traps 56–57
trench foot 85
tripwire 57
trousers 21

underground shelters *63*
underwear 19
uniform
  Australian SAS *11,* 12, *23*
  Canadian Special Forces 22

Vietnam War *8,* 11–12

war *see* fighting
washing 86
wasps 88
water 10
  bottles for carrying 37
  contaminated 41
  lack of 35–36
  purifying water 26,
  34, 39–41
  solar stills 27, 38
  spotting signs of 37–38
  transpiration bags 38–39
weapons
  catapults 75
  clubs 69–71
  FN FAL rifles *8*
  knives 33, *73,* 75
  M16 rifles *15*
  spears 74
weather 22, 64–65, 85
webbing *37*
web sites 94
whistles 78
wire saws 27
wood tools *71*
World War II
  Australian SAS 10
  Canadian Special
  Forces 13